WHEN WILL THE SNOW TREES GROW?

 Ben Shecter

A Charlotte Zolotow Book

An Imprint of HarperCollins*Publishers*

Library of Congress Cataloging-in-Publication Data
Shecter, Ben.
    When will the snow trees grow? / written and illustrated by Ben
Shecter.
        p.   cm.
    "A Charlotte Zolotow book."
    Summary: By celebrating all the changes that autumn brings to the
land, a bear passes on his knowledge about the cycles of life to a young
boy as they each prepare for their own separate winter.
    ISBN 0-06-022897-0. — ISBN 0-06-022898-9 (lib. bdg.)
    [1. Autumn—Fiction.   2. Bears—Fiction.]   I. Title.
PZ7.S5382Wg   1993   92-32557
[E]—dc20   CIP
                                                                 AC

Typography by Christine Kettner
1   2   3   4   5   6   7   8   9   10
❖
First Edition

To Joe and Mollie

 WHEN will the snow trees grow?

AFTER the pumpkins are harvested,
And the leaves change color.

AND the wind blows around the house.
When the chimneys are cleaned,
And the logs are cut, split,
and stored.

WHEN the warm quilts are
taken from the closet,
along with sweaters and coats.

WHEN cold lemonade doesn't
taste as sweet.
And the darkness comes early.
And the cricket's song is soft.

THEN will the snow trees grow?

NO, we have more time
until they grow. . . .

WHEN the pumpkins are
turned to pie,
And when the leaves fall upon
the ground,

And the wind blows inside
the house,
And when the smoke curls from
the chimney,

And the fireplace is good
to be near,

WHEN the quilts are on the beds,

A<small>ND</small> the sweaters and coats are comfortable to wear,

WHEN hot chocolate is the most delicious thing to drink,

AND when there is a quiet,
And you can feel the first frosty
flake upon your face,

THEN you will know
it is the time
snow trees grow.